The Magic School Bus ®
TO THE RESCUE
EARTHQUAKE

D0378373

SCHOLASTIC INC.

New York   Toronto   London   Auckland   Sydney
Mexico City   New Delhi   Hong Kong   Buenos Aires

The author would like to thank Robert de Groot
of the Southern California Earthquake Center and California
Institute of Technology for his help in reviewing the manuscript.

Written by Gail Herman.

Illustrations by Hope Gangloff.

Based on *The Magic School Bus* books
written by Joanna Cole and illustrated by Bruce Degen.

ISBN 0-439-42938-2

12 11 10 9 8 7 6 5 4 3   4/0   5/0   6/0

Designed by Peter Koblish

Printed in the U.S.A.   40

First printing, January 2003

INTRODUCTION

Hi, my name is Phoebe. I am one of the kids in Ms. Frizzle's class.

Maybe you've heard of Ms. Frizzle. (Sometimes we just call her the Friz.) She is a terrific teacher, but she's a little weird . . . very different from the teachers at my old school. When we learn about science, she usually takes us on a field trip in the Magic School Bus.

Believe me, it's not called *magic* for nothing. No other bus can do the things this one can!

We know we're going on a field trip when Ms. Frizzle comes to class wearing wacky new clothes — like a dress covered in dinosaurs, or moon earrings. And we can usually guess where we're going, because her clothes are a clue.

But one day she came to class wearing a plain blue dress. No designs, no pictures. She wasn't even wearing earrings! Talk about strange. Here's what happened. . . .

CHAPTER 1

"*Pssst,* Phoebe! What's going on with the Friz this morning?" Wanda whispered.

"I don't know," I answered.

Ms. Frizzle was acting awfully weird. First she gave us a spelling test. Next she took us to the school library. Then we had recess.

Spelling, library, and recess. That's it! And now we were all sitting quietly at our desks. Ms. Frizzle stood in front of the classroom, holding a pointer, just like an ordinary teacher.

I hoped she was feeling okay.

"I can't believe this!" I whispered to Wanda. "It's just like my old school."

"All right, class," Ms. Frizzle said. "Today we are learning about the earth. It is made up of three parts: the crust, the mantle, and the core."

Finally! I thought. *Science! Get ready for something strange.* Everyone sat up straight, expecting something . . . anything!

But Ms. Frizzle only pulled down a chart.

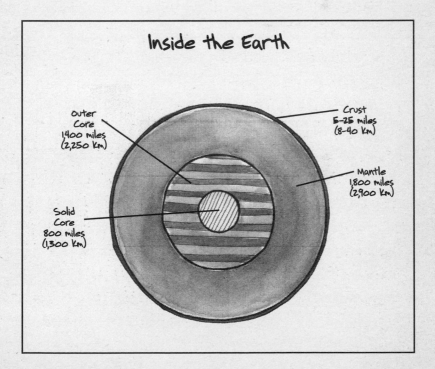

Inside the Earth

Outer Core
1,400 miles
(2,250 km)

Crust
5-25 miles
(8-40 km)

Mantle
1,800 miles
(2,900 km)

Solid Core
800 miles
(1,300 km)

"Inside the earth, it is hot. And the deeper inside you go, the hotter it gets."

She pointed to the center. "This is the core — and it is all metal. The metal in the outer core is melted and runny."

"You mean like the chocolate bar I kept in my back pocket once?" Wanda asked. "When I put the chocolate inside my pocket, it was cool. It wasn't soft at all. But by the time I took it out, the chocolate was all warm and melted."

"Exactly!" said Ms. Frizzle. "That's what the metal is like. Now let's look at the inner core. The very hottest part of Earth."

"How hot is that?" asked Ralphie.

"Well, it's about 10,000 degrees Fahrenheit."

Dorothy Ann — or D.A., as we call her — waved her hand. She had about six books spread out on her desk. And she was checking through each one. "That's the same temperature as the surface of the sun!"

"You're right, D.A. It's so hot in the inner core," the Friz continued, "that its metal is

4

melted, too. But the other layers of the earth press down on it, so it seems solid under all that weight."

"Are we going to swim through the liquid metal wearing special diving suits?" Carlos asked. He was expecting to go on a wild field trip, too.

"And test the temperature of the inner core with giant thermometers?" Tim added.

But Ms. Frizzle only pointed to another layer. "The mantle is made out of rock. Most of it is solid. But the inside part is melted into a thick goo called magma."

"Wow," said Wanda. "I can't believe that rock can melt, too!"

"Ms. Frizzle!" Keesha called out. "Will we use the Magic School Bus to drill inside the earth? So we can slosh through the magma wearing heat-proof boots?"

Ms. Frizzle laughed. "Not today, Keesha." Then she moved her pointer. "The top layer of the earth is the crust. It's made up of rock, too."

D.A. pulled out another book and flipped

through the pages. "Excuse me, Ms. Frizzle. Do we walk on the crust?"

I thought D.A. was asking about another field trip. You know, would we tiptoe on a giant pie crust or something. But it turns out the crust is just the ground under our feet. And D.A. knew it.

"Your research is absolutely correct!" Ms. Frizzle said. "The crust includes all of the earth's surface. The mountains, the valleys, and all the ocean beds."

Arnold leaned back in his chair and grinned. "Nothing to be nervous about today. I don't think we're going on a field trip at all!"

No field trip? In Ms. Frizzle's class?

D.A. happily scribbled away in her notebook. Arnold kept grinning. He hates going on field trips, but everyone else was disappointed.

"Is it just me," Ralphie whispered, "or does anyone else feel a little . . . bored?" He yawned and sneaked a peek at a comic book.

"Super Sam, superhero to the rescue!" he read to himself, turning a page.

Ms. Frizzle didn't seem to notice. She went on talking and pointing. "The earth's crust feels solid to us, but it is divided into about thirty pieces. The pieces fit together almost like a puzzle. These giant pieces are called plates — tectonic plates."

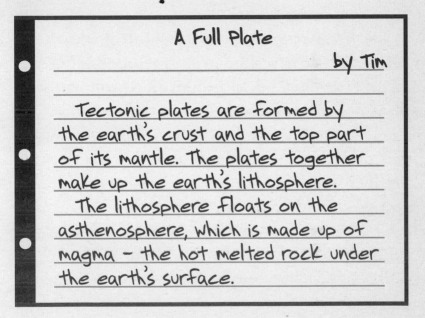

A Full Plate

by Tim

Tectonic plates are formed by the earth's crust and the top part of its mantle. The plates together make up the earth's lithosphere.

The lithosphere floats on the asthenosphere, which is made up of magma - the hot melted rock under the earth's surface.

"These plates hold land and oceans, just like dinner plates hold food," Ms. Frizzle told us. "And they carry the land and oceans when they move, just like you carry food on a plate.

7

But oceans and continents are big and it takes years for the plates to travel just a few inches. This movement is called continental drift."

D.A.'s hand shot up again. She waved a book in the air. "Listen to this! It says here that scientists think all the continents were once stuck together. They were one big giant mass of land called Pangaea. But then the mass split into pieces and drifted apart."

D.A. showed us a picture from her book. It was hard to believe that the plates had moved the continents all that way.

"And the plates are still in motion," Ms. Frizzle said. "Let's find out why these plates are on the move in the first place."

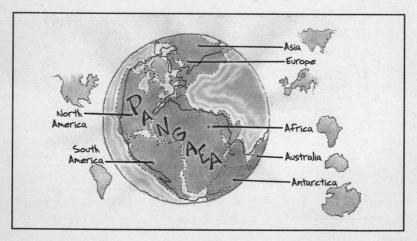

Oh, that's our field trip, I thought. *Ms. Frizzle will turn the* bus *into a tectonic plate!*

But she only pulled down another chart. "Remember part of the mantle is made of magma? And the magma is always flowing, so it pushes and pulls the plates as it moves. This makes the plates bump and scrape and press against one another. And they can pull away from one another."

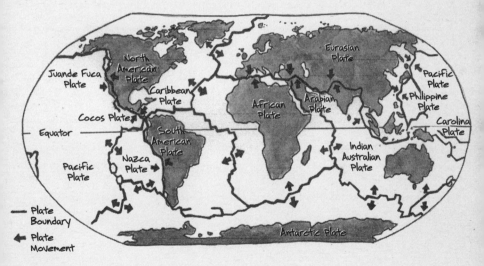

Keesha shook her head. "But that means the ground is always moving!"

Ralphie put down his comic book. He

lifted his feet from the classroom floor. "I don't feel a thing," he said.

"We don't usually feel the earth moving," the Friz explained, "because it moves about as fast as your fingernails grow."

Wanda studied her nails. "I can't see them getting longer. But I know they do."

Ms. Frizzle nodded. "Sometimes, though, we do feel the earth move."

Arnold gulped. "I don't like the sound of this," he muttered.

"The magma pulls and pushes the plates all the time, and sometimes two plates wind up wedged together so they push against each other. They're pushing so hard in fact, they get stuck in that position."

"I got it!" Ralphie flipped to a page in his comic book. "It's like Super Sam arm wrestling his archenemy, Mean Gene. They're both superstrong. So nobody wins. Nobody pins down the other one's arm, because nobody can move!"

Keesha said, "Until one gets tired and gives up, and that makes them both topple over!" She looked confused. "But does something like that happen with the earth?"

"In a way," said the Friz. "There are lots of reasons the earth moves. Rocks can slide past each other. Or they can rub against each other, then break and fall into new positions.

"But when the rock is superstrong — like Ralphie's superheroes — and the plates push each other, they just keep stretching. The pressure builds and builds. Finally, it gets to be too much. The rock snaps. And all that energy is set loose — through the weakest point in the earth's crust."

D.A. reached for another book. "This book says the weakest point is called a fault!"

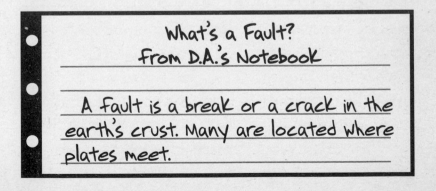

What's a Fault?
from D.A.'s Notebook

A fault is a break or a crack in the earth's crust. Many are located where plates meet.

"Righto, D.A.," said the Friz. "The energy that is released when there is movement on a fault is called seismic energy. The energy from the shock waves is so explosive, the ground shakes, shudders, and cracks."

Arnold said, "That sounds just like an . . ."

"Yes, Arnold?" said Ms. Frizzle.

"Earthquake?" Arnold spoke so softly I could hardly hear him.

"Did you say earthquake, Arnold?"

"Um," Arnold stammered. "Uh, maybe I said, uh, milk shake?"

"No, no, no." Ms. Frizzle shook her head. "You were exactly right, Arnold. Earthquake. To the bus, everyone!"

From the Desk of Ms. Frizzle

Our planet is always changing. Mountains grow. Land shifts. Plates move closer together and farther apart. Using their knowledge about the earth and the way it moves, scientists say Los Angeles and San Francisco will be next to each other in about 15 million years.

CHAPTER 2

"We were having such a nice time in the classroom," Arnold said sadly. "Why, oh, why, do we have to go on a field trip?"

"Not just any field trip," Carlos joked as we trooped onto the bus. "An earthshaking one!"

Liz, the class lizard, was already waiting for us. She was peering at an electronic map on the dashboard. Then she pressed a button and a red circle lit up.

"That must be the earthquake site," I told Wanda.

"Thank you, Liz," said the Friz. "Seat belts, everyone!"

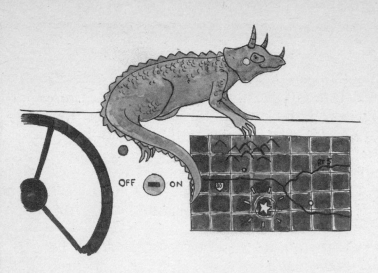

I waited for the Magic School Bus to sprout wings. I thought we would take off like an airplane. But the bus just drove down one road, then another, and another. It was a long ride. I think everyone fell asleep. I know I did.

"Wake up, class!" Ms. Frizzle finally said. "We're here!"

I opened my eyes. We had stopped in front of an ordinary-looking office building. EARTHQUAKE CENTER read a sign out front.

"What's going on?" Tim nudged Carlos. "I don't hear any loud rumbles. I don't see the earth splitting open."

Where Earthquakes Happen

Over ninety percent of all earthquakes happen where plates meet. The following are the ways in which all earthquakes occur:
- When plates push together
- When plates grind past each other
- When plates pull apart
- When rock is very weak, often in the middle of a plate
- When magma rises up from under a plate, known as a hot spot

"We're at an Earthquake Center?" Arnold crowed. "Not an earthquake? This is going to be an ordinary field trip!"

We walked inside the building. A woman came over. She smiled at the Friz. "Hello, Valerie."

We all giggled. It's funny to hear your teacher's first name.

"Class," Ms. Frizzle said. "This is Dr. Quivers. She's a geophysicist."

"Geo-what-is-ist?" asked Ralphie.

"Geophysicist," D.A. repeated. "That's a scientist who uses gravity, electricity, and magnetism to study the earth —"

"And earthquakes!" finished Dr. Quivers. "Let's go on our tour."

We walked around a large open office. To tell the truth, it didn't seem that different from a regular office. There were telephones and computers, and people hurrying around with papers.

Arnold was grinning again.

What's the Chance There'll Be an Earthquake Today?

by Tim

One hundred percent! In fact, there's a 100 percent chance of an earthquake all 365 days of the year. There are thousands each and every day, and millions in a year. Luckily, most are too small to feel. About 60 a year are large enough to cause damage.

Keesha gazed around. "So what do you do here, exactly?"

"Well, one important thing we do is bring lots of people together — people who do different jobs and can help out before, during, and after an earthquake," said Dr. Quivers.

"Like who?" I asked.

"Seismologists, for one. The word comes from Greek, meaning 'to shake.' Those are the scientists who study the shock waves inside the earth. Then there are engineers who can help rebuild the area. Local emergency forces for search and rescue. We help everyone stay in touch," said Dr. Quivers.

Wanda walked over to a huge map on the wall. "Cool map," she said.

"It's really a computer screen," Dr. Quivers explained. "And it shows earthquakes almost as soon as they happen, all over the world. The bigger the circle around an area, the greater the earthquake. New information goes into the map every 30 minutes."

Ms. Frizzle pointed to a different computer. "Here's another map, class."

17

"That just shows the United States," Wanda said.

"Right," said Dr. Quivers. "That's the United States Geological Survey site. People can log on to a website named 'Did you feel it?'. People can input information after they feel the ground shake. Then it appears on the map. The scientists working here can learn a lot from the information people give."

"I hope my street's not on that map," Arnold said under his breath.

Where's It Shaking?
by Wanda

Every state has had an earthquake. Florida and North Dakota have had the fewest, and Alaska has had the most.

The largest recorded earthquake in the United States struck Prince William Sound, Alaska, on March 27, 1964. Its moment magnitude was 9.2.

Something bothered me. "Excuse me, Dr. Quivers," I said. "People who feel an earthquake put information on that website. But can any of these computers tell when an earthquake happens, by figuring it out for themselves?"

"Yes, these computers can keep track of tremors, when the earth shakes just a little. Sometimes the earth moves the tiniest bit — too little for us to see or feel — but these computers know it."

"How?" Tim asked.

"The computers are linked to instruments in the field."

"Field? Like a baseball field?" Ralphie twisted his baseball cap.

"Field means outside, places where earthquakes can happen. The different instruments send information back to computers about what is happening in the earth. One example is the Global Positioning System, or GPS."

Wanda squinted at all the computers. "That's pretty cool, but can the GPS tell you when an earthquake is about to happen?"

How GPS Works

by Tim

There are hundreds of GPS stations throughout the world. Antennae from these stations are connected to satellites and send signals through cable wires to computers all the time.

GPS can measure the size of an earthquake by examining how much a station was moved during a seismic event. It compares its position before the quake to where it is after the quake.

Dr. Quivers shook her head. "I wish it could. But right now, there isn't a way to predict that. An earthquake is like stretching a rubber band."

Carlos nudged Tim. He picked up a rubber band from a nearby desk. Then he stretched it, more and more.

Tim said, "Stop it! It's going to break."

"It's okay," Carlos said, watching the rubber band as he pulled it longer, "I've got time to —"

Snap!

"Ow!" Carlos shook his hand. "That smarts!"

"Thank you for the smart demonstration," Ms. Frizzle put in. "We could tell that the rubber band would break. But we didn't know when."

A Series of Shaky Events
by Carlos

Earthquakes often come in a series. Foreshocks are smaller earthquakes that come before the largest earthquake in the series. The largest quake is called the mainshock. Not all earthquakes have foreshocks.

Aftershocks are earthquakes that follow the largest shock of the series. They are smaller shocks, and there can be many of them.

Dr. Quivers laughed. "That's the way it is with earthquakes, too. Even though he couldn't guess *when* it would break, I'll bet Carlos could probably guess *where* the rubber band would break: the place where it was stretched the most. In studying earthquakes, we can guess where the ground will break — in places where the plates rub together and are pulled and stretched. But we can't say when exactly."

"What do you do if you think an earthquake is coming?" I asked.

"We try to prepare. We call local governments that can ready emergency teams. The real work comes when there is an earthquake. Then we send people to the field to check instruments we have at the location and to see the effects. And, of course, we measure the magnitude."

"Magnitude?" I repeated.

Tim picked up a booklet from another desk and flipped through it. "That means how big the quake is."

The Size of the Shock
by Tim

For decades, the size, or the magnitude, of earthquakes has been measured with the Richter scale. The scale starts at zero and includes decimal points.

The higher the number is, the stronger the earthquake. An earthquake that measures 2 or under is called a microquake. It is small enough that people usually can't feel the vibration. In a 4.5 quake you can feel the ground shake. By 6, the earthquake is so strong, buildings can collapse. Each time the number increases by 1.0 on the scale, the ground shakes ten times faster. The earthquakes with the highest magnitude measure about 9 on the scale, and they are devastating.

"That booklet has lots of good information," said Dr. Quivers. "But recently, scientists have developed a more exact measure of earthquakes: the moment magnitude scale. It also uses a number scale, but it can measure the actual energy released in an earthquake. Moment magnitude is figured using electronic equipment. It helps scientists measure small differences in the biggest earthquakes."

"How on earth did scientists measure earthquakes before computers?" Carlos wanted to know.

"They used a machine called a seismograph," Dr. Quivers said.

I wasn't used to being on normal field trips, and my mind started to wander.

As Dr. Quivers began to explain, my feet began to wander, too. I headed over to a machine to examine some big rolls of paper. They looked a little like huge rolls of toilet paper, with a pen on top. I knew it had to be some sort of special machine.

"Watch out for Sniffer!" Dr. Quivers called to me.

I peered at the equipment. *Is that a Sniffer?* I wondered.

The Machine Is a Seismograph
by Keesha

Before electronics, the seismograph recorded the size of the vibrations of the earth to help scientists figure out the strength of earthquakes.

The seismograph is a drum covered with paper. The drum is always spinning. When the earth moves, the pen makes a wavy line on the paper. The longer the wavy lines and the closer they are together, the stronger the earthquake.

5.6   2.7

"It's an old machine, but it still works," Dr. Quivers continued.

"Oh!" I realized the machine was a seismograph. Not a sniffer, whatever that was. The pen on top looked pretty fragile. I didn't want to hurt it, so I backed away. But then I bumped into something else. Something big and solid.

"Oops!" I stumbled and landed with a thud on the floor. Slowly, I lifted my head. I was nose to nose with a German shepherd. But the dog didn't blink an eye. She didn't even open an eye. She was fast asleep, snoring.

So that's a Sniffer!

CHAPTER 3

"Ohhh!" I breathed softly. I didn't want to wake up Sniffer. But she must have known I was there. She opened one eye, then the other.

"Hi, Sniffer."

She pushed her nose into my hand. I scratched her behind the ear. Her tail thumped. But she didn't stand up. She just yawned and put her head between her paws.

"Sniffer seems so tired!" I said.

"Well, she's just a little old." Dr. Quivers came closer. "Sniffer used to be a rescue dog. But now she doesn't work anymore. She's retired."

Doggone Good Workers
by Phoebe

Special handlers train rescue dogs every day for at least a year. The handler and dog have to be very close for the training to work. Sometimes the dog learns through play: tug-of-war or ball or pretend rescue. So the best dogs for rescue work love people and playing! Usually, they are larger breeds like German shepherds, golden retrievers, or Labrador retrievers. Most begin training when they are puppies.

"You mean she used to save people?" Keesha asked. "If they got trapped? Or hurt in an earthquake?"

"That's right. Sniffer worked as part of a rescue team. An important part. Rescue equipment can't see through concrete. And listening devices don't always work. But Sniffer

29

could pick up people's scents — even when they were buried under buildings. And she could lead rescuers to the right place."

"Wow!" said Ralphie. He waved his comic book in the air. "Super Sam could use a dog like that. Super Sniffer to the rescue! She could be a superhero!"

"Not a superhero," said the Friz. "Sniffer is a *real* hero!"

Sniffer stretched. Then she settled to the floor again. She looked so sad. I wanted to make her feel better. How could we help?

I had it!

"Ms. Frizzle!" I tugged on the Friz's sleeve. "I bet Sniffer feels bad she's not helping anyone. That she's not doing any more rescues."

"Go on, Phoebe," Ms. Frizzle said, smiling.

"I know we're having an ordinary field trip and all —" I continued.

"So?" Arnold put in. "What's wrong with an ordinary field trip?"

I ignored him. "But please, please can

we take Sniffer to a place where she used to help? So she can remember the important work she did?"

"Are you serious?" Arnold asked. "You really want to go to a place that gets earthquakes?"

I nodded. "Please?"

Ms. Frizzle opened her mouth to answer. But then we all heard a beeping sound. The map on a computer screen had changed. A red circle had appeared!

"Uh-oh," said Dr. Quivers. "We just got word that there are nearby vibrations. It may be a foreshock."

Shocking News
by Keesha

When there is an earthquake, scientists cannot tell if it is a foreshock or the mainshock. They have to wait to see if there are later, stronger earthquakes.

"Well, Phoebe." Ms. Frizzle pointed to the circle on the map. "This is where the earthquake happened. It's very close by. Do you still want to take Sniffer on a field trip?"

"No!" said Arnold.

"Yes!" I said.

"Then we're off to the site of an earthquake! Class, let's get cracking!"

CHAPTER 4

Dr. Quivers waved good-bye to us and rushed over to the computer. She was so busy she didn't realize that we didn't leave alone. We had a super Sniffer with us!

We all raced into the bus. Liz stood on the hood. Then she waved a checkered flag. The bus flattened into a race car as Liz jumped in, too.

"On your mark," called the Friz. The engine revved.

"Get set." She put the race car into gear. "Go!"

Whoosh! We were speeding down the road. Seconds later, we whizzed through a small town. I saw buildings, a park, a bridge. We drove by so fast, it was all a blur.

We slowed down a bit as we left the town. On our way out, I read a sign. THANK YOU FOR VISITING RATTLESBURG. COME BACK SOON!

A few minutes later, the Magic School Bus braked to a stop. It stretched back into its normal shape.

"Here we are!" said Ms. Frizzle.

Everyone stepped off the bus. Sniffer gave one excited yelp. And then she settled down by my feet and yawned.

"Are you sure this is the right place?" I asked.

D.A. checked a map she had taken from the center. "We're just east of Rattlesburg. And just west of Shaker Springs. I guess we're right in the middle of nowhere!"

"Not exactly!" said Ms. Frizzle happily.

We all looked around. We were standing in some sort of valley. Steep rocky hills rose up from either side of the road. It sure felt like the middle of nowhere.

I couldn't see much of anything. The

ground was dry. There was hardly any grass. And no people.

I sighed. Sniffer had her head between her paws once again. So far, nothing was happening. And this wasn't helping her one bit.

"You might think there's not a lot to see," Ms. Frizzle continued. "But this is our epicenter."

"Epicenter? Is that anything like the Earthquake Center?" Carlos said.

So Many Centers!
by Ralphie

An earthquake begins at the hypocenter – it is where the shift or break in the rock happens. That could be more than 550 miles (885 km) below the earth's surface!

The epicenter is the spot on the earth's surface that is right above the hypocenter.

Ms. Frizzle smiled. "No, but it is related to the hypocenter!"

Epicenter, hypocenter, whatever center. This was it? The place the earth shook? It all seemed so quiet!

"Okay!" Arnold rubbed his hands together. "Thanks for showing us the sites, Ms. Frizzle. Time to go!"

But I wasn't ready to go. I still couldn't see any sign of seismic activity. And Sniffer still didn't look happy. "Is there anything else we can show Sniffer?" I asked Ms. Frizzle. "You know, to make her feel better?"

The Friz led us to a different spot. There, I could see a long, long tear in the ground. Little mounds of dirt lined either side.

"Here's the fault," said Ms. Frizzle.

"Whoa, so the fault actually tore its way all the way up to the surface?" Wanda said.

"That's what happened here," the Friz confirmed. "But not all faults break to the surface during a quake. And a crack is not necessarily always along a fault."

Question: Why Does California Have So Many Earthquakes? Answer: It's the San Andreas Fault's Fault!

by Wanda

The famous San Andreas Fault is the border between two tectonic plates: the Pacific Plate and the North American Plate. It's the longest fault in an amazing system that includes many smaller faults. It runs more than 800 miles (1,287 km) long — through most of California! Most faults are far underground, but you can see the tears and ripples of the San Andreas Fault system on the earth's surface for miles.

* Main Epicenter
— San Andreas Fault Zone

Pacific Ocean

San Francisco

Menlo Park

Highway 17
Santa Cruz Area

N

"Oh, come on, Ms. Frizzle." Carlos laughed. "It's nobody's fault."

"Carlos," we all groaned as he snickered to himself.

"Don't crack up over your own joke," Tim added.

"This is all very interesting," I interrupted. "But what about Sniffer?" I scratched Sniffer behind the ear. She licked my hand.

"I know what we can do! I'll hide, then let Sniffer find me. That should cheer her up."

"Good thinking, Phoebe," said the Friz. "It might remind her of her rescue days."

Keep Those Tails Wagging
by Arnold

Sometimes during search missions, rescue dogs have trouble finding people. To keep the dogs in good spirits, dog handlers will hide so their dogs can find them. The dogs are cheered up and ready to keep working!

Wanda put her arm around Sniffer and gently faced her away from me. Then I raced across the fault and ducked behind a big rock.

"Come on, Sniffer," said Wanda. "Where's Phoebe? Go get Phoebe, girl!"

I peeked around the rock. Sniffer's ears lifted. Her nose twitched. She leaped into action, bounding across the ground. In seconds she stood over me.

"Ruff!" she called to the others. She wagged her tail. Then she gave me a lick.

"Good girl," I said.

We walked back to Ms. Frizzle. Sniffer stood straighter. She looked much more alert.

Ms. Frizzle checked her watch. "We have time for one more round of hide-and-dog-seek."

"Okay now." I rubbed my hands. "Who wants to hide next?"

By now, the other kids were roaming around the fault. Only Arnold stood close to Ms. Frizzle. It was a little spooky here, so I couldn't blame him.

"Arnold?" I said. "It's your turn."

"Why is it always me? But I guess the faster I hide, the faster we'll go home."

I covered Sniffer's eyes with my hands. Arnold tiptoed away.

"Ready," he called. He ducked behind another big rock.

This time, Sniffer worked even faster. She found him in no time at all.

"Okay, Phoebe?" Arnold asked, running toward the Friz and me. "Can we go home now?"

"Rufff!" Sniffer bounded into the air, following at Arnold's heels.

"Well, Sniffer seems much happier," I said. "I guess I'm ready to leave."

"To the bus, everyone!" Ms. Frizzle called out.

The other kids stopped exploring. "Okay, Ms. Frizzle," Wanda shouted back.

Liz opened the doors.

"Gee," said Ralphie as everyone began walking. He took out his Super Sam comic, ready to read again. "Nothing much happened here at the fault. This really was an ordinary field trip."

Everyone got on board. Before I got on, too, I turned to Sniffer. "Remember this," I told her. And I showed her the fault one last time.

Parkfield, California: Earthquake Capital of the World
by Keesha

If you think the earthquake capital would be along the San Andreas Fault, you're right. Parkfield has lots of small earthquakes every year. And earthquakes that register between a 5 and 6 magnitude strike there about every 20 years.

All at once, a loud rumbling noise filled the air. The ground shook. Harder and harder. I tried to keep my footing. But I felt like I was surfing.

"Earthquake!" shouted Arnold.

CHAPTER 5

"Hurry, Phoebe." Ms. Frizzle was already behind the wheel. "As I always say, when the earth rocks, it's time to roll!"

The earth was really moving now. It pitched me forward. I fell to my knees. Stumbling, I grabbed Sniffer's collar. Two more steps and we reached the bus, but the ground was shaking so much, I couldn't manage to climb the stairs. Just then, a hand reached out, and Keesha pulled Sniffer and me into the bus.

The Magic School Bus bucked like a bronco. I could hardly sit in the seat. It was an actual earthquake. A major one!

Catch the Wave!
From D.A.'s Notebook

Starting from the hypocenter (the place where the seismic energy is released), the quake fans out through the earth in waves. First come primary (or P) waves. They can make a loud roaring noise and squeeze the earth up in bunches. Next come shear (or S) waves. They will make the ground shake from side to side. Finally we feel the surface waves. A surface wave is an earthquake wave that is trapped near the earth's surface.

The ground shook hard. Noise filled the air.

The Magic School Bus sprouted blades on the roof. *Whirr! Whirr!* It was a helicopter!

I peered out the rattling window. We were almost ready for liftoff.

Rumble, rumble. One giant rock shook loose from the hilly slope. It rolled toward us, picking up speed.

Rumble, rumble. I spun around to check the window across the aisle. Another huge rock swayed back and forth. It began to roll, too! Faster and faster. The rocks rushed toward us from opposite directions!

"Oh, bad. Oh, bad. Oh, bad," said Keesha.

And then we took off! Just below us, the rocks crashed together. Bits and pieces flew everywhere.

Look Out Below!
by Carlos

Earthquakes can jerk rocks and soil from the sides of mountains. The rocks slide down, moving faster and faster, gathering more soil along the way, until – boom! – it all crashes to the ground. Avalanche!

"That was close!" said Ralphie. "I'd hate to be the center of a rock sandwich!"

Wanda put her hands over her ears. "When is this earthquake going to end?"

We were flying toward Rattlesburg. Below us, a section of highway buckled. One car slid off the road to safety. Then the entire road cracked in half. Bricks tumbled from buildings. Some collapsed in a heap of dusty smoke. Streetlights fell. Signs toppled.

And then everything fell quiet. The Magic School Helicopter's gentle whir was the only sound we heard.

The earthquake was over.

Ms. Frizzle pulled a stopwatch out of her pocket and pressed a button. "Fourteen seconds," she announced.

The earthquake lasted only 14 seconds! It seemed to go on forever.

"Amazing," agreed D.A. "I read that many earthquakes last only 10 to 15 seconds. But a lot can happen in that short time." She pointed to the ground. "Just look!"

We all pressed against the windows.

Rattlesburg was a mess. Pieces of wood and bricks covered the streets. Buildings were half standing. Sidewalks and roads were cracked and broken.

"Ruufff!" Sniffer lunged for the door. She was ready for action.

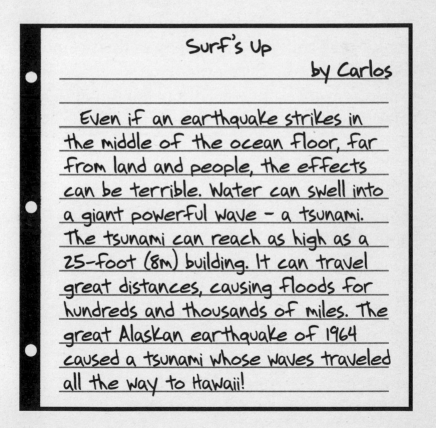

Surf's Up

by Carlos

Even if an earthquake strikes in the middle of the ocean floor, far from land and people, the effects can be terrible. Water can swell into a giant powerful wave – a tsunami. The tsunami can reach as high as a 25-foot (8m) building. It can travel great distances, causing floods for hundreds and thousands of miles. The great Alaskan earthquake of 1964 caused a tsunami whose waves traveled all the way to Hawaii!

"Not yet, Sniffer," I said, holding her back.

Helicopters circled the area. Fire engines, police cars, and ambulances raced through the torn-up streets.

First Things First
by Wanda

Right after the earthquake has stopped, firefighters turn off all power and gas lines. Cracked or broken gas pipes and dangling wires can lead to out-of-control fires. In the big 1906 San Francisco earthquake, hundreds more people died from fires than from the earthquake itself!

Looking down, I could see car and truck doors swing open. All at once, the place buzzed with activity. People swarmed everywhere.

"The search and rescue workers are here," the Friz called. "They're setting up headquarters in that big grassy park, clear of falling buildings and debris."

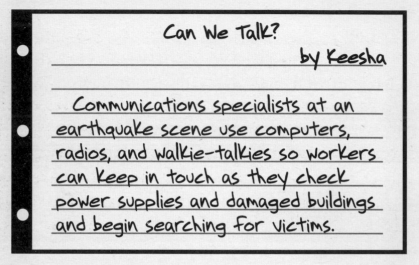

Can We Talk?

by Keesha

Communications specialists at an earthquake scene use computers, radios, and walkie-talkies so workers can keep in touch as they check power supplies and damaged buildings and begin searching for victims.

From our helicopter perch, we could see everything. Dozens of people jumped out of one truck.

Sniffer whimpered and pressed her nose against the window, watching.

"Easy does it, girl," I told her. "I know you want to help the workers. I do, too."

Now workers were pulling on helmets, goggles, boots, and gloves.

"They look like mutants from Super Sam Comic number 29," said Ralphie.

"They're wearing special gear," Ms. Frizzle explained, "that won't catch on fire and helps keep them safe."

Next the workers strapped on backpacks. "I know they're not going camping," said Carlos. "But those must be filled with some sort of supplies."

"Splendid deduction, Carlos. The packs are filled with first-aid kits, water, food, oxygen — for the people who have been buried under wreckage, or for the workers, too, if they get stuck," Ms. Frizzle said.

The men and women slipped on knee pads and elbow pads.

"To protect them as they crawl through small spaces," Keesha guessed.

"Excellent!" Ms. Frizzle nodded.

Emergency medical workers sprang from ambulances. Some began to set up tents in the big open space. Others organized bandages, blankets, and blood supplies, getting ready to treat people who'd been hurt.

More workers brought out smaller tents and giant pieces of heavy plastic. They hauled out crates of food and water jugs. People had lost their homes. They'd need food and shelter.

Do We Have Any Band-Aids?
by Wanda

Logistics specialists keep track and organize more than 16,000 pieces of equipment — from concrete-cutting saws to search cameras to medical supplies.

So much was going on, nobody noticed the Magic School Bus land near the other helicopters.

"Stay clear of the workers so they can do their job. Observe the action, class," Ms. Frizzle directed.

"Just observe?" Arnold perked up. "Nothing else?"

"I wish there was something we could

do!" Wanda said, disappointed. She pointed to Sniffer. "She wants to do something, too!"

I held Sniffer by the collar. "Ruuuufff!" She strained, pulling me away from the others.

"Arf!" A team of rescue dogs stood in a semicircle with their handlers.

"Roooof!" Sniffer ran up, wagging her tail. The dogs wagged back. But they stayed close to their handlers.

"Easy does it, boy," one woman said. "You're going to do great." The woman and her dog seemed awfully close.

"Come on, Sniffer," I insisted. "These dogs are waiting for instructions."

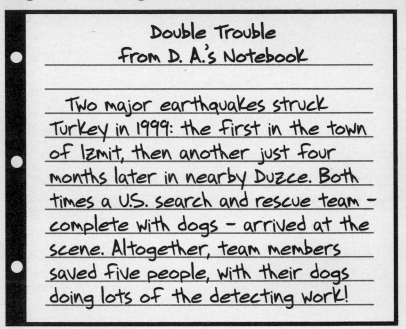

Double Trouble
from D. A.'s Notebook

Two major earthquakes struck Turkey in 1999: the first in the town of Izmit, then another just four months later in nearby Duzce. Both times a U.S. search and rescue team – complete with dogs – arrived at the scene. Altogether, team members saved five people, with their dogs doing lots of the detecting work!

I led Sniffer back to Ms. Frizzle and the others. They were standing near a group of rescue workers.

The team leader spread a map on a table. "Okay. We've figured out the places where we should start our searches. Now we can assign a rescue squad to each area."

Another worker nodded. "Good thing

this happened on a weekday morning. Most people are away from town, working in the big city close by."

The leader divided everyone into smaller groups. Then she pointed to different areas on the map and told each group where to go.

She nodded at one group. "Listen up. This is important. There's an elementary school three blocks away. It seems to be in pretty good shape. It's still standing. But it's filled with children and teachers."

Immediately, the group took off.

Maybe now we could help. I looked at Ms. Frizzle. Ms. Frizzle looked at me.

"Okay, class," she announced. "It's back to school!"

"Our school?" Arnold asked hopefully.

"No way, Arnold," I said. Sniffer wagged her tail. "Rattlesburg Elementary — for a lesson in earthquake rescue!"

CHAPTER 6

We walked quickly toward the school.

"Hey, Pheebs," said Tim. "Nice outfit."

I glanced down. I was wearing protective clothing and gear. "Take a look at yourself, Tim," I shot back. We all wore the same heavy clothes, goggles, and helmets.

"I wouldn't go to an earthquake without the proper attire." Ms. Frizzle patted her helmet. "Always dress for distress, I say."

Nobody stopped us as we walked. We looked just like a rescue team.

It was a short distance away. But it was tough going. Sidewalks slanted. Broken glass littered the street. All around us, response teams worked.

Volunteers stepped up to a big apartment building — or what used to be a big apartment building. Each one joined a line and began passing a huge bucket filled with rubble to the next in line. It seemed like an old-fashioned way to clear the mess. But it was definitely working.

I couldn't believe how much had happened in just fourteen seconds.

I stepped over a torn awning that read, RUSTY'S RESTAURANT. It was on the first floor of another half-collapsed building.

"Hey!" Carlos looked around the place. "This restaurant is still in one piece. Maybe we can get a burger since we already had a shake."

"Not so fast," said the Friz. "Even search and rescue workers can't go in. It needs to be checked first."

Is It Safe Inside?
by Arnold

Part of the rescue engineers' job is to check buildings for safety. Are they stable? Or could there be more swaying? And if some of the building has collapsed, will clearing the rubble affect the other parts? To do this, engineers check floor plans – maps of the insides of buildings – and test the strength of the building materials.

As she spoke, a man and woman examined a wall. "They're engineers," Ms. Frizzle explained. "They're making sure the building won't collapse further."

Measuring a Building – the Earthquake Way
by Wanda

Sometimes engineers have already placed instruments inside buildings. These strong motion recorders measure how the building responds during an earthquake – how much it has moved – and compares that to the motion of the ground beneath it. Many schools, hospitals, homes, and highways in high-earthquake areas have these recorders. The recorders show how well buildings hold up during quakes. Then engineers and architects figure out if they can be built even better!

We could see signs on some buildings telling people to keep out.

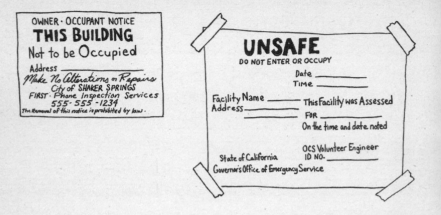

"This area's all clear," an engineer called.

"Could be trouble over here!" another engineer shouted. She pressed against a wall. It seemed to give a bit.

Immediately, more workers were on the scene. Everyone moved quickly but carefully. They knew people might be trapped inside the building. Any moment now, more of the building could give way. But workers, too, need to be safe.

They carried long beams of wood to the building. They jammed the beams under the sagging section to prop it up.

"All shored up!" a woman shouted.

Now two other workers entered the building. They held small devices.

"Are those search and rescue workers?" Tim asked.

"Nope," said the Friz. "They're hazardous-materials specialists. They're making sure no dangerous gases were released during the earthquake. The environment has to be safe."

A specialist gave a thumbs-up sign. "Now searchers can go inside!" Wanda said.

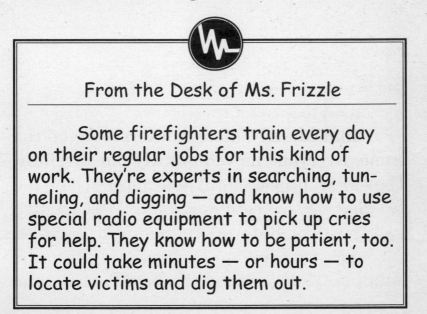

From the Desk of Ms. Frizzle

Some firefighters train every day on their regular jobs for this kind of work. They're experts in searching, tunneling, and digging — and know how to use special radio equipment to pick up cries for help. They know how to be patient, too. It could take minutes — or hours — to locate victims and dig them out.

In a flash, firefighters hurried over.

Finally, we approached the school. Sniffer pulled me toward the doors, ready for action. All at once, she stopped. Then she looked back at me, puzzled. The school looked perfectly fine.

"This building must be earthquake-resistant," Ms. Frizzle said. "It's in good shape."

Buildings That Bend Don't Break
by Carlos

In some areas that get lots of earthquakes, architects design quake-resistant buildings. They use materials that can bend — steel, for instance. Bricks would fall apart during an earthquake. But steel would sway. Some skyscrapers are built on special springs or have rubber material in their foundations so they sway with vibrations, too.

Rescue workers led children out one by one. Across the street in a big field, medical workers had set up a tent and were checking everyone for injuries.

The kids looked frightened and excited at the same time. But no one seemed hurt.

One boy, though, seemed awfully upset. Sniffer pulled me closer to him.

Now I could see the boy was trying to stay calm. He was taking lots of deep breaths. But tears kept running down his cheeks. He tugged on his bright red hair nervously.

"My cat, Sunshine!" he blurted to a firefighter. "I don't know if he's okay!"

"What's your name?" the firefighter asked the boy.

"Will."

"I bet your cat is doing just fine, Will. But we need to make sure you're fine, too. Go with your class to the tent. Doctors are waiting to talk to you."

Will swallowed, as if he had a big lump in his throat. "But do you know anything

about Oak Street? That's where I live. Are the houses still standing?"

"Hey!" somebody called to the firefighter. "There are more kids over here!"

The firefighter turned back to Will. "I can't say for certain, Will. And I need to go now. But workers are doing their best to make sure everyone is safe. I'm sure you'll hear news about your cat soon."

The firefighter hurried away. Still sniffling, Will walked slowly toward the tent with the others.

Poor Will. Sniffer whimpered, as if she understood. I started to follow Will, to make sure he was okay.

"Come along, Phoebe!" Ms. Frizzle called from across the school yard. "We have more observing to do!"

CHAPTER 7

At first, Sniffer wouldn't budge. But I pulled gently on her collar, and we caught up to our class.

Down the block from the school, big trucks were hard at work. Bulldozers pushed away rubble from a fallen building. Cranes were lifting heavier chunks of stone and metal.

Workers still bustled about. And people wandered here and there, almost in a daze.

Sniffer wasn't very interested. She kept pulling me back toward the field by the school.

"What is it, girl?" I asked. "What's wrong?" Maybe she knew something.

"Ms. Frizzle," I begged. "Can we please go back to the school rescue tent?" I told her about Will and his cat, Sunshine. "Can we please check on him?"

"Very well, Phoebe. As I always say, where there's a will, there's a way. Class!" Ms. Frizzle waved toward the tent. "This way!"

I found Will's class right away. Doctors were still examining the kids. And teachers were getting information about their parents and families. I looked around. I didn't see Will anywhere.

Sniffer yelped loudly.

"Is that your rescue dog?" one girl said to me. "You're lucky you know she's safe. One boy in our class was so worried about his cat, he just ran home."

"Will!" I cried. "He's going home! Ms. Frizzle! He could get in big trouble. We have to find him!"

The Friz whistled for Liz to start the Magic School Helicopter. We all raced aboard.

Moments later, we hovered above Rattlesburg, over the neighborhood close to the school.

"He said he lives on Oak Street," I remembered.

Liz pressed some buttons on the dashboard. A Rattlesburg map came up on the small computer screen. An arrow appeared, pointing to one place: Oak Street!

"Hold on to your rescue helmets!" the Friz shouted. We zipped above the houses, turning left, and left again.

Survivor Story
by Phoebe

Rescue workers arrive on the scene as quickly as they can. Chances are, victims buried under the wreckage would not survive much longer than two days. They would die from lack of food or water. Or they would be injured so badly by flying bricks or falling beams that they could not make it.

Still, there is always hope: Many workers remember rescues of people buried longer. In the August 1999 earthquake in Turkey, a four-year-old boy was saved after spending six days under debris!

"There it is!" the Friz cried. The helicopter dropped close to the ground.

All at once, I spotted a red-haired boy. Will! He stood in front of a small two-story

house. The front porch sagged and windows were broken. But that was all.

"Sunshine!" he called. "Come on out. It's me, Will. Come out!" He waited a moment. Nothing happened. "Sunshine!" This time he really shouted, and his voice cracked with fear.

"Ruuuf!" Sniffer barked, then scrambled out of the copter and landed lightly on her feet.

"I'm going, too!" I said. "I have to warn Will." The copter landed, and I jumped out.

"I'm coming in after you, Sunshine!" Will shouted.

D.A. called out to me, "He'd better be careful. There could be an aftershock!"

After Earthquakes Come Aftershocks
from D.A.'s Notebook

After an earthquake, rocks under the crust readjust, causing more shaking. These aftershocks are smaller than the mainshock, but they can cause buildings that are already damaged to collapse. Aftershocks can happen minutes, hours, even days after an earthquake. You never know.

Before Will could move, I heard a rumble. All around us, buildings shook and swayed.

"Aftershock!" I shouted.

I gazed at Will's house. The porch broke completely away from the house. Shingles fell from the roof.

Will stood still, not moving a muscle. Then he started for the house again.

"Wait!" I said, running over with Sniffer. "You can't go in there! It may not be safe!"

"But my cat —" Will began.

"I know your cat might be inside," I continued. "I know you want to rescue him."

Sniffer lifted her head at the word *rescue*. She rose up on her hind legs to lick my face. Then she took off, leaping through an open window — into the house!

"Sniffer!" I cried. I wanted to get her out of there. Back outside where it was safe. I wanted to help Will, too. But we couldn't go into the house. Not yet.

I grabbed Will's hand. Then I pulled him on board the helicopter.

"Are you a rescue worker?" Will shouted.

I didn't have time to answer. There could be another aftershock at any minute.

"Ms. Frizzle. We have to do something!"

I glanced at the rest of the class. They looked determined, too. Even Arnold nodded.

"All right, class!" Ms. Frizzle said. She reached for a button on the dashboard.

The Magic School Helicopter began to spin. It spun faster and faster, and shrank smaller and smaller — with us inside! By the time we stopped spinning, the bus was no bigger than a mouse.

WHOAH!

put put
squeak!

"We have to find Sniffer and Sunshine. We have to go inside!" I shouted, but my voice came out a squeak.

Then I noticed a tail where the emergency exit in the back of the bus used to be. And there were whiskers by the windshield. The bus was a mouse!

"Protective shield up!" said the Friz. She pressed another button and a clear screen dropped over the Magic School Mouse like armor.

Will's mouth dropped open. "Are you guys for real? Or did this earthquake rattle my brain?"

"We're going to help you find Sunshine," I told him.

"This is the strangest rescue team I've ever seen," he said. "But if you think you can get Sunshine out of there, let's go!"

We scurried through a broken window and into the house.

"Sniffer up ahead!" said the Friz. We stopped suddenly in the living room, behind an overturned table.

From the Desk of Ms. Frizzle

What To Do in Case of an Earthquake

If You Are Indoors:
- Take cover under a piece of furniture — a big desk or table — and hold on to it tightly. Stay away from windows and glass.
- Do not go outside. Objects could be falling all around.

If You Are Outside:
- Find a clear area away from buildings, trees, and wires — and stay there.

If You Are in a Car:
- Stay away from bridges, overpasses, and tunnels. Stop in a safe area, and stay in your car.

Everyone Should:
- Stay calm.
- Listen to emergency information on a battery-operated radio or TV.
- Watch out for aftershocks.

Teachers! Please Take Note!
- Do not take your class into earthquake-damaged buildings. Only Ms. Frizzle is allowed to do that!

Books, dishes, and vases covered the floor.

"Sniffer?" I squeaked from the Magic School Mouse. She looked around. "It's me, Phoebe!"

Curious, she sniffed the bus.

Smile! You're on Camera!

by Tim

Sometimes special cameras and microphones are strapped onto rescue dogs. The equipment sends back sounds and pictures to workers, who can pinpoint the location of trapped people.

"I hope she doesn't think we're lunch," moaned Arnold.

"Not Super Sniffer, Superhero!" Ralphie said.

"Let's get to work, girl," I said. "Let's find Sunshine!"

CHAPTER 8

Sniffer put her nose to the ground. She circled the living room. Then she padded toward a doorway.

All at once, another aftershock hit. *Crash! Boom!* A lamp smashed to the ground. Then, quiet. It was over as soon as it started.

"The house could be even weaker now," said the Friz. "We may not have much time."

Sniffer climbed a rickety pile of books. The Magic School Mouse zipped after her. Then we stopped.

The refrigerator had fallen, blocking the way to the kitchen. To us, it looked like a mountain.

Sniffer scrambled up.

"Here goes!" said the Friz. She changed gears. The tiny Magic School Mouse roared like a lion. Then it soared up the pile after Sniffer.

On the other side, Sniffer waited. Once again, she put her nose to the ground. Then she sniffed up to the back door and out onto another porch.

Big holes gaped in the porch slats. Whole planks were missing. Sniffer jumped from side to side. The Magic School Mouse scampered around the openings. Finally Sniffer stopped, her head cocked to one side.

"Ruuuf!" She pawed at one of the planks. "Sunshine must be there," I said. I wanted to help so bad! I jumped out of my seat to get a better look.

Will jumped up, too.

"Hold on, you two," said Ms. Frizzle.

The Magic School Mouse edged close to the hole. Its nose poked over the edge.

"Meow!"

"I hear mewing!" Wanda said.

"Ruuuf!" Sniffer barked.

"It's Sunshine!" Will shouted. "She's in that hole!"

We all peered through the front windows. A bright orange cat cowered in the dust and dirt. He shivered, but he seemed fine.

"How do we get him out of there?" asked Wanda. "He looks too scared to move."

"Easy!" said Ms. Frizzle. "I never knew a cat to say no to a mouse chase. But first I think Sniffer needs to give him some space."

"Sniffer!" I called out. "Meet us in front of the house!"

"Yip!" Sniffer dashed away.

"All right," said the Friz. "On the count of three. One . . . two . . . three —"

"Squeak!" everyone shouted, Will loudest of all.

Sunshine lifted his head.

"He sees us!" cried Arnold.

Sunshine's eyes lit up. The bus spun around, and Sunshine leaped out of the hole.

We zoomed around the backyard, then down the driveway with Sunshine in hot pursuit.

Sniffer was waiting for us in front of the house. *Squeak!* The Magic School Bus Mouse turned back into a regular-size bus, and we all tumbled out.

Sunshine froze, surprised. "It's okay, Sunshine," Will said quickly as he leaped down the bus stairs. "I'm here. Everything's going to be okay."

"Meow!" Sunshine wound himself around Will's legs. Then Will scooped him up.

How a Dog Rescue May Work
by Wanda

The dog handler takes off the dog's leash. He or she instructs the dog in a quiet voice to start the search. The dog moves away slowly, sniffing, trying to nose out a scent. When the dog runs in circles around a certain area, the handler knows someone has been found. The dog barks and paws at the earth in one spot. That's a signal for workers to dig, or to use listening devices to locate anyone buried in the rubble. Then the dog and partner move on to another area.

"Ruuuff!" Sniffer moved closer. She softly nosed the cat.

Ms. Frizzle clapped her hands. "Phone, please, Liz. We need to call the teachers at your school, Will, and tell them you're okay.

I'm sure they've been in touch with your parents, too. Then we should head back."

"Sunshine, too?" Will asked.

The Friz nodded. "There's a veterinarian at the rescue tent, to help if a rescue dog is hurt. I'm sure the doctor would be happy to check Sunshine."

"Thank you!" said Will. "I can't wait to see my parents. They'll be so glad that Sunshine is okay. They can fix the house up easy — it's really just the porches and windows. The important thing is that Sunshine's safe!"

A little while later, we were back by the school. We all watched Will walk over to the vet's tent. Across the field, he gave us a thumbs-up sign.

I grinned. "Sunshine really is fine. Good girl, Sniffer."

Sniffer was so happy, she chased her tail around and around.

I turned to the Friz. "You know, Ms. Frizzle, Sniffer is just fine, too. I think it's time to bring her home."

CHAPTER 9

Once again, the Magic School Bus turned into a helicopter. We lifted off the ground . . . away from the damaged buildings . . . the broken streets and sidewalks . . . the bright white tents . . . the workers and trucks.

In no time at all, we were back at the Earthquake Center. The Magic School Helicopter spun around and around, dropping into the parking area and whirling into a regular bus.

"Ruuuff!" Sniffer bounded outside — right into Dr. Quivers.

"Whoa!" said Dr. Quivers. She looked at

us a little strangely. "I was wondering where you'd gone to. And you have Sniffer!" Dr. Quivers patted Sniffer's head. "That's unbelievable. Sniffer hardly leaves the building!"

Then Dr. Quivers bent down to see eye to eye with her dog. "Hey, you seem different! More like your old self. If I didn't know any better, I'd say you'd been to an earthquake!"

We all laughed.

"But that would be impossible!"

"Of course it would," Ms. Frizzle said.

"A lot of the staff is actually off to that earthquake site right now," Dr. Quivers continued. "We have to report on the damage. Talk to engineers. See if any buildings can be saved. Plus we need to check some equipment that's kept nearby."

People were loading equipment and computers into the back of a truck.

"All set, Dr. Quivers," one called. "Ready to go!"

Sniffer wagged her tail, then begged.

"What? You want to come, too?" Dr. Quivers smiled.

Earth to Scientists: Come in, Please
by Ralphie

Before and after an earthquake, scientists check instruments to measure changes under the ground.

The strainmeter is an instrument that measures the stretching and the squeezing of the ground near active faults. How high was the pressure before the earthquake? How much pressure has been let go? This information helps scientists learn more about that particular earthquake – and could help them figure out how much strain these rocks can take before another earthquake strikes.

The tiltmeter is an instrument that measures changes in the land, its slopes and slants. Has the land changed since the earthquake? How much?

"Ruuf! Ruuff!"

"Well, you never know when a rescue dog can come in handy."

Dr. Quivers turned to another worker. "We're taking Sniffer with us!"

"We should be leaving now, too," Ms. Frizzle said. "Thank you for the tour and all the information."

"You're welcome."

"Good-bye!" everyone called out.

"Good work, Super Sniffer," Ralphie whispered. "You really should be in a comic book — right next to Super Sam."

Then I put my arms around Sniffer and nuzzled her neck. I was so proud of her!

"Good-bye, girl. I'll miss you. But I'm glad you're happy."

We all stepped back on the bus. I peered out the window. Sniffer was nipping excitedly at Dr. Quiver's heels.

Arnold looked out, too. "Well, now that we're on our way home, I have to say I'm glad this wasn't an ordinary field trip."

"Me, too." I glanced at the Friz. She was

driving the Magic School Bus, humming loudly.

I shook my head. "I knew it would be a real Magic School Bus field trip from the start. Really. How could it have been any other way?"

Earthquake Severity

This chart lists the possible effects of earth-quakes with different magnitudes.

Richter Scale Magnitudes	Earthquake Effects
Less than 3.5	Shock generally not felt, but recorded.
3.5–5.4	Shock often felt, but rarely causes damage.
Under 6.0	At the most, earthquake causes slight damage to well-designed buildings. It can cause major damage to poorly constructed buildings that are close by.
6.1–6.9	Earthquake can be destructive in areas up to about 60 miles (100 km) from epicenter.
7.0–7.9	This is a major earthquake. It can cause serious damage over larger areas.
8 or greater	The power of this earthquake is great. It can cause serious damage in areas several hundred miles across.

The largest earthquake ever recorded was in Chile in 1960 (magnitude: 9.5).

Check out these other Magic School Bus To The Rescue books:

Forest Fire
Blizzard